Great Start!

Purchased with
Smart Start Funds

Someone's Come to Our House

Written by **KATHI APPELT**

Illustrated by **NANCY CARPENTER**

EERDMANS BOOKS FOR YOUNG READERS

GRAND RAPIDS, MICHIGAN   CAMBRIDGE, U. K.

Published 1999 by Eerdmans Books for Young Readers

An imprint of Wm. B. Eerdmans Publishing Co.

255 Jefferson Ave. SE

Grand Rapids, Michigan 49503

P.O. Box 103, Cambridge CB3 9PU U.K.

Printed in Hong Kong

05 04 03 02 01 00 99   7 6 5 4 3 2 1

Library of Congress Cataloging-in-Publication Data

Appelt, Kathi, 1921-

Someone's Come to Our House / written by Kathi Appelt; illustrated by Nancy Carpenter.

p. cm.

Summary: The members of a family celebrate the arrival of a new baby.

ISBN 0-8028-5144-4 (alk. paper)

(1. Babies - Fiction. 2. Family life - Fiction. 3. Stories in rhyme.) I. Carpenter, Nancy, ill. II. Title.

PZ8.3.A554So 1998

(E) - dc21   98-46965

                    CIP

                    AC

The illustrations were done in oil on gessoed Bristol board.

The text type was set in MrsEavesBold.

The book was designed by Willem Mineur.

To the Liles family:

Cathy, Ben, Benjamin,

Marisa & Garrison

— *K. A.*

To the new Keaton arrival

— *N. C.*

Someone's come to our house.
Yes, yes, bless-a-my-soul!
Bright new start,
Brand new heart—
Come and see at our house.

Friends and kin, come on in.
My, my, bless-a-my-soul!
Faces shine,
Special time—
Come join in at our house.

Grandpa calls one and all.
Oh, oh, bless-a-my-soul!
    Waves us in
    With a grin—
Come gather now at our house.

Papa beams, eyes agleam.
See, see, bless-a-my-soul!
Stands up tall,
Welcomes all—
Come and hug at our house.

Granny bakes angel cakes.
Mmm, mmm, bless-a-my-soul!
Homemade stew,
Biscuits, too—
Come and share at our house.

Brother laughs, laughs out loud.
Hey, hey, bless-a-my-soul!
    Happy beat,
    Dancing feet—
Come be glad at our house.

Sister smiles, sunny child.
Shine, shine, bless-a-my-soul!
    Tickly toes,
    Sister glows—
Come and play at our house.

Mama sings, softly sings.
Sweet, sweet, bless-a-my-soul!
    Lullabies,
    Gentle sighs—
Come and sing at our house.

Angels keep watch so deep.
Peace, peace, bless-a-my-soul!
Stories tell.
All is well.
Come give thanks at our house.

Love's at home in our house.
Yes, yes, bless-a-my-soul!
Baby's here.
God is near.
Come rejoice at our house.